SUCCESSORIES®

Great Quotes
from
Great Women

Compiled by Peggy Anderson

Illustrated by Michael McKee

CAREER PRESS
3 Tice Road, P.O. Box 687
Franklin Lakes, NJ 07417
1-800-CAREER-1
201-848-0310 (NJ and outside U.S.)
FAX: 201-848-1727

SUCCESSORIES: GREAT QUOTES FROM GREAT WOMEN

Cover design by The Hub Graphics Corp.

Printed in the U.S.A. by Book-mart Press

To order this title, please call toll-free 1-800-CAREER-1 (NJ and Canada: 201-848-0310) to order using VISA or MasterCard, or for further information on books from Career Press.

Library of Congress Cataloging-in-Publication Data

Great quotes from great women / [compiled by Peggy Anderson].
        p.   cm. -- (Successories)
     ISBN 1-56414-288-4 (pbk.)
     1. Quotations, English. 2. Women--Quotations.   I.
Anderson,
     Peggy. II. Series.
     PN6081.5.G74 1997
     808.88'2--dc21   96-51678
                                                              CIP

Dedicated with love and gratitude to my mother, Mary Crisorio, and my mentor, Ann Gilchrist.

Preface

Great women are not considered so because of personal achievements, but for the effect their efforts have had on the lives of countless others. From daring feats of bravery to the understated ways of a compassionate heart, great women possess a common strength of character. Through their passion and persistence, they have advanced womanhood and the world.

The insights herein come from major female influencers of the arts, entertainment, science, politics, religion, law, medicine, social causes and sports. Some figures are well known; others are the unfamiliar names of unsung heroes. While each deserves our deepest consideration, the selected group of profiles features pioneers in their fields, crusaders for humanity and catalysts of change.

These are timeless examples of individuals unafraid to challenge the status quo. These are lives and words worth remembering.

ELEANOR ROOSEVELT
1884 - 1962

Eleanor Roosevelt was a United Nations diplomat, humanitarian and wife of President Franklin D. Roosevelt. During her 12 years as First Lady (1933-1945), the unprecedented breadth of her activities and her advocacy of liberal causes made her nearly as controversial a figure as her husband. She showed particular interest in such humanitarian concerns as child welfare, slum clearance projects and equal rights.

After President Roosevelt's death (1945), President Harry Truman appointed her a delegate to the United Nations, where, as chairman of the UN Commission on Human Rights, she played a major role in the drafting and adoption of the Universal Declaration of Human Rights.

Eleanor Roosevelt was one of the most widely admired women in the world and remains an inspiration to many.

"It is better to light a candle than to curse the darkness."

"No one can make you feel inferior without your consent."

Great Quotes from Great Women

"It is not fair to ask of others what you are not willing to do yourself."

"The future belongs to those who believe in the beauty of their dreams."

"The only thing that makes one place more attractive to me than another is the quantity of heart I find in it."

Jane Welsh Carlyle, 1801 - 1866
Scottish poet

"But men never violate the laws of God without suffering the consequences, sooner or later."

Lydia M. Child, 1802 - 1880
American abolitionist, writer and editor

"I listen and give input only if somebody asks."

Barbara Bush, 1925 -
Former First Lady of the U.S. and humanitarian

"Light tomorrow with today."

Elizabeth Barrett Browning, 1806 - 1861
English poet

"It is easy to be independent when you've got money. But to be independent when you haven't got a thing, that's the Lord's test."
Mahalia Jackson, 1911 - 1972
American Gospel singer

"Mistakes are part of the dues one pays for a full life."
Sophia Loren, 1934 -
Italian actress

"I think the key is for women not to set any limits."
Martina Navratilova, 1956 -
Professional tennis player

"Follow your instincts. That's where true wisdom manifests itself."
Oprah Winfrey, 1954 -
American actress and talk show host

SUSAN B. ANTHONY
1820 - 1906

Susan B. Anthony is best remembered as a pioneer and crusader of the women's suffrage movement in the U.S. As president of the International American Suffrage Association, her work helped pave the way for the 19th Amendment to the Constitution, giving women the right to vote.

Discouraged by the limited role women were allowed in the established temperance movement, Anthony helped form the Woman's State Temperance Society in New York, one of the first organizations of its kind.

From 1856 to the outbreak of the war in 1861 she served as an agent for the American Anti-Slavery Society. Organizing the International Council of Women in 1888 and the National Woman Suffrage Alliance in 1904, Susan B. Anthony was a major catalyst for social change in America and abroad.

"Men their rights and nothing more; women their rights and nothing less."

"Failure is impossible."

"...The day will come when man will recognize woman as his peer, not only at the fireside, but in councils of the nation. Then, and not until then, will there be the perfect comradeship, the ideal union between the sexes that shall result in the highest development of the race."

HELEN KELLER
1880 - 1968

Helen Adams Keller was born in Tuscumbia, Ala., in 1880. A severe illness in infancy left her deprived of sight, hearing and the ability to speak.

Through the constant and patient instruction of Anne Sullivan, Helen Keller not only learned to read, write and speak, but went on to graduate cum laude from Radcliffe College in 1904. In addition to becoming the author of several articles, books and biographies, she was active on the staffs of the American Foundation for the Blind and the American Foundation for the Overseas Blind. She also lectured in over 25 countries and received several awards of great distinction.

Helen Keller's courage, faith and optimism in the face of such overwhelming disabilities stand as a symbol of human potential.

"Keep your face to the sunshine and you cannot see the shadows."

"I thank God for my handicaps, for through them, I have found myself, my work and my God."

"Security is mostly a superstition. It does not exist in nature, nor do the children of men as a whole experience it. Avoiding danger is no safer in the long run than outright exposure. Life is either a daring adventure or nothing."

"We've chosen the path to equality; don't let them turn us around."

Geraldine A. Ferraro, 1935 -
The first woman nominated as vice president of the U.S.

"There were angry men confronting me and I caught the flashing of defiant eyes, but above me and within me, there was a spirit stronger than them all."

Antoinette Brown Blackwell, 1825 - 1921
The first woman in the U.S. to be ordained as a minister; feminist and writer

"The brain is not, and cannot be, the sole or complete organ of thought and feeling."

Antoinette Brown Blackwell, 1825 - 1921
American minister, feminist and writer

"When so rich a harvest is before us, why do we not gather it? All is in our hands if we will but use it."
Elizabeth Ann Seton, 1774 - 1821
The first American saint

"You can't give people pride, but you can provide the kind of understanding that makes people look to their inner strengths and find their own sense of pride."
Charleszetta Waddles, 1912 -
American nun and writer

"I've never sought success in order to get fame and money; it's the talent and the passion that count in success."
Ingrid Bergman, 1915 - 1982
Swedish actress and playwright

MARGARET THATCHER
1925 -

Margaret Thatcher was the first woman in European history to be elected prime minister.

Thatcher ran for Parliament in 1950, but it was not until 1959 that she was finally elected to the House of Commons. She served as parliamentary secretary to the Ministry of Pensions and National Insurance, and later as secretary of state for education and science. She was elected the leader of the Conservative Party in 1975, and the party's victory in the 1979 elections elevated her to the office of prime minister.

Margaret Thatcher became known as the Iron Lady because of dedication to the ideals in which she believed.

"You may have to fight a battle more than once to win it."

"What is success? I think it is a mixture of having a flair for the thing that you are doing; knowing that it is not enough, that you have got to have hard work and a certain sense of purpose."

"Let our children grow tall, and some taller than others if they have it in them to do so."

"To wear your heart on your sleeve isn't a very good plan; you should wear it inside, where it functions best."

"I wasn't afraid to fail. Something good always comes out of failure."
Anne Baxter, 1923 - 1985
American actress

"I am not a has-been. I'm a will-be."
Lauren Bacall, 1924 -
American actress

"Many a humble soul will be amazed to find that the seed it sowed in weakness, in the dust of daily life, has blossomed into immortal flowers under the eye of the Lord."
Harriet Beecher Stowe, 1811 - 1896
American writer

"If you have made mistakes, even serious ones, there is always another chance for you. What we call failure is not the falling down, but the staying down."

Mary Pickford, 1893 - 1979
American actress

"Yes, I have doubted. I have wandered off the path, but I always return. It is intuitive, an intrinsic, built-in sense of direction. I seem always to find my way home. My faith has wavered but saved me."

Helen Hayes, 1900 - 1993
American actress and writer

MOTHER TERESA
1910 -

Mother Teresa, born Agnes Gonxha Bojarhiu, is revered for her lifelong dedication to the poor, most notably the destitute masses of India.

In 1928, at the age of 18, she went to Ireland to join the Institute of the Blessed Virgin Mary, and shortly thereafter traveled to India to work with the poor of Calcutta. After studying nursing, she moved into the slums of the city and founded the Order of the Missionaries of Charity. In 1971 Mother Teresa was awarded the first Pope John XXIII Peace Prize. By the late 1970s, the Missionaries of Charity numbered more than 1,000 nuns who operated 60 centers in Calcutta and over 200 centers worldwide.

Mother Teresa's selfless compassion and devotion to the destitute earned her the Nobel Peace Prize in 1979.

"We can do no great things—only small things with great love."

"I am a little pencil in the hand of a writing God who is sending a love letter to the world."

"I do not pray for success. I ask for faithfulness."

"Loneliness and the feeling of being unwanted is the most terrible poverty."

"I have learned from experience that the greater part of our happiness or misery depends on our dispositions and not on our circumstances."

Martha Washington, 1732 - 1802
Former First Lady of the U.S.

"The artist has always been and still is a being somewhat apart from the rest of humanity."

Beatrice Hinkle, 1874 - 1953
American psychiatrist and writer

"When you get into a tight place and it seems you can't go on, hold on, for that's just the place and the time that the tide will turn."

Harriet Beecher Stowe, 1811 - 1896
American writer

"Where large sums of money are concerned, it is advisable to trust nobody."

Agatha Christie, 1891 - 1975
English writer

"We fought hard. We gave it our best. We did what was right and we made a difference."

Geraldine A. Ferraro, 1935 -
The first woman nominated as vice president of the U.S.

"We have learned that power is a positive force if it is used for positive purposes."

Elizabeth Dole, 1936 -
U.S. Labor Secretary

MARIE CURIE
1867 - 1934

Polish-born French physicist Marie Curie was famous for her work on radioactivity. From childhood, she was remarkable for her prodigious memory and intellect.

One of Curie's outstanding achievements was to have understood the need to accumulate intense radioactive sources, not only for the treatment of illness, but also to maintain an abundant supply for research in nuclear physics. Shortly after this discovery, however, Marie Curie died from leukemia caused by the action of radiation.

Twice a winner of the Nobel Prize, Marie Curie made immense contributions to physics because of her influence on subsequent generations of nuclear physicists and chemists.

"One never notices what has been done; one can only see what remains to be done."

"Nothing in life is to be feared. It is only to be understood."

"You cannot hope to build a better world without improving the individuals. To that end each of us must work for his own improvement, and at the same time share a general responsibility for all humanity, our particular duty being to aid those to whom we think we can be most useful."

"The more visible signs of protest
are gone, but I think there is a
realization that the tactics of the
late-60s are not sufficient to meet
the challenges of the 70s."
Coretta Scott King, 1927 -
American lecturer, writer and Civil Rights activist

"All talk of women's rights is
moonshine. Women have every
right. They have only to exercise
them."
Victoria Claffin Woodhull, 1838 - 1927
First woman nominated to the presidency of the U.S.

"The soul can split the sky in two
and let the face of God shine
through."
Edna St. Vincent Millay, 1892 - 1950
American poet and writer

"If I had one wish for my children, it would be that each of them would reach for goals that have meaning for them as individuals."

Lillian Carter, 1898 - 1984
Mother of President Jimmy Carter

"I don't need a man to rectify my existence. The most profound relationship we'll ever have is the one with ourselves."

Shirley MacLaine, 1934 -
American actress and writer

"People who fight fire with fire usually end up with ashes."

Abigail Van Buren, 1918 -
American newspaper columnist and lecturer

HARRIET TUBMAN
1820 - 1913

Born a slave in Maryland, Harriet Tubman yearned to be free. In 1849, she made her escape to Pennsylvania through the Underground Railroad. She then used that route 19 more times, returning to the South to lead more than 300 slaves to freedom.

As the years passed, Tubman became known as the "Moses" of her people, directing them out of enslavened land. During the Civil War, she served the Union Army as a nurse and a spy.

Following the war, Tubman raised funds to construct schools for ex-slaves. She labored for female suffrage and, in 1903, established a shelter for poor, homeless blacks. An American heroine, Harriet Tubman is remembered as an extraordinary humanitarian.

"I had reasoned this out in my mind, there were two things I had a right to: liberty and death. If I could not have one, I would have the other, for no man should take me alive."

"I should fight for my liberty as long as my strength lasted, and when the time came for me to go, the Lord would let them take me."

"I had crossed the line, I was free; but there was no one to welcome me to the land of the freedom. I was a stranger in a strange land."

"Superior people never make long visits."
Marianne Moore, 1887 - 1972
American poet

"The battle to keep up appearances unnecessarily, the mask—whatever name you give creeping perfectionism—robs us of our energies."
Robin Worthington, 1932 -
American writer

"There's a period of life when we swallow a knowledge of ourselves and it becomes either good or sour inside."
Pearl Bailey, 1918 - 1990
American singer

"Laziness may appear attractive, but work gives satisfaction."
Anne Frank, 1929 - 1945
German diarist

"Habits do not like to be abandoned, and besides, they have the virtue of being tools."
Charlotte Painter, 1926 -
American writer

"I realized that if what we call human nature can be changed, then absolutely anything is possible. From that moment, my life changed."
Shirley MacLaine, 1934 -
American actress and writer

JANE ADDAMS
1860 - 1935

Jane Addams was an American social reformer and pacifist who won the Nobel Prize for Peace in 1931.

She is probably best known as the founder of Hull House in Chicago, one of the first social settlements in North America. A boarding club for working girls, Hull House offered college-level courses in various subjects and instruction in art, music and crafts. In addition to services and cultural opportunities for the largely immigrant population, Hull House trained young social workers in the practical aspects of the field.

Addams worked with labor and other reform groups for the first juvenile court law, tenement house regulations, an eight hour working day for women, factory inspection and worker's compensation.

Jane Addams committed her life to justice for immigrants and blacks, equal rights for women and to the struggle against poverty in the U.S.

"Unless our conception of patriotism is progressive, it cannot hope to embody the real affection and the real interest of the nation."

"Civilization is a method of living, an attitude of equal respect for all men."

"In his own way each man must struggle, lest the normal law become a far-off abstraction utterly separated from his active life."

"Success can make you go one of two ways. It can make you a prima donna, or it can smooth the edges, take away the insecurities and let the nice things come out."
Barbara Walters, 1931 -
American journalist, writer, television producer and commentator

"Life begets life. Energy creates energy. It is by spending oneself that one becomes rich."
Sarah Bernhardt, 1844 - 1923
French actress and writer

"The way I see it, if you want the rainbow, you gotta put up with the rain."
Dolly Parton, 1946 -
American singer, songwriter and actress

"New links must be forged as old ones rust."
Jane Howard, 1935 -
American writer

"Imagination is the highest kite one can fly."
Lauren Bacall, 1924 -
American actress

"When people say: she's got everything, I've only one answer: I haven't had tomorrow."
Elizabeth Taylor, 1932 -
American actress and humanitarian

"Not truth, but faith, it is that keeps the world alive."
Edna St. Vincent Millay, 1892 - 1950
American poet and writer

SANDRA DAY O'CONNOR
1930 -

Sandra Day O'Connor's career helped advance the status of women in politics and law.

A graduate of Stanford Law School, Day was an assistant attorney general for Arizona. In 1969, this modern conservative became a Republican member of the Arizona Senate, in which she became the majority leader—the first woman in the U.S. to hold such a position.

Her election as a Superior Court judge in Maricopa County was followed by an appointment to the Arizona Court of Appeals.

When President Ronald Reagan appointed Sandra Day O'Connor to the U.S. Supreme Court in 1981, she became the first woman to ever sit on the High Court.

"We pay a price when we deprive children of the exposure to the values, principles and education they need to make them good citizens."

"I don't know that there are any short cuts to doing a good job."

"The family unit plays a critical role in our society and in the training of the generation to come."

"Each of us brings to our job, whatever it is, our lifetime of experience and our values."

"The pain of leaving those you grow to love is only the prelude to understanding yourself and others."

Shirley MacLaine, 1934 -
American actress and writer

"Careful grooming may take 20 years off a woman's age, but you can't fool a long flight of stairs."

Marlene Dietrich, 1901 - 1992
German/American actress and singer

"Hungry people cannot be good at learning or producing anything, except perhaps violence."

Pearl Bailey, 1918 - 1990
American singer

"A happy woman is one who has no cares at all; a cheerful woman is one who has cares, but doesn't let them get her down."

Beverly Sills, 1929 -
American opera singer

"Parents can only give good advice or put [children] on the right paths, but the final forming of a person's character lies in their own hands."

Anne Frank, 1929 - 1945
German diarist

"Don't confuse being stimulating with being blunt."

Barbara Walters, 1931 -
American journalist, writer, television producer and commentator

MARGARET MEAD
1901 - 1978

American anthropologist Margaret Mead's great fame owed as much to the force of her personality and outspokenness as it did to the quality of her scientific work. As an anthropologist, she was best known for her studies of the nonliterate peoples of Oceania, especially with regard to various aspects of psychology and culture, the cultural conditioning of sexual behavior, natural character and culture change.

As a celebrity, she was widely known for her forays into such far-ranging topics as women's rights, child-bearing, sexual morality, nuclear proliferation, race relations, drug abuse, population control, environmental pollution and world hunger.

"If we are to achieve a richer culture— one rich in contrasting values— we must recognize the whole gamut of human potentialities, and so weave a less arbitrary social fabric, one in which each diverse human gift will find a fitting place."

"We are living beyond our means. As a people, we have developed a life style that is draining the earth of its priceless and irreplaceable resources without regard for the future of our children and people all around the world."

"The most exciting thing about women's liberation is that this century will be able to take advantage of talent and potential genius that have been wasted because of taboos."

Helen Reddy, 1941 -
Australian/American singer and songwriter

"We are concerned not only about the Negro poor, but the poor all over America and all over the world. Every man deserves a right to a job or an income so that he can pursue liberty, life and happiness."

Coretta Scott King, 1927 -
American lecturer, writer and Civil Rights activist

"Art is not for the cultivated taste.
It is to cultivate taste."
Nikki Giovanni, 1943 -
American poet, author and lecturer

"I have crossed over on the backs
of Sojourner Truth, Harriet
Tubman, Fannie Lou Hamer and
Madam C. J. Walker. Because of
them I can now live the dream.
I am the seed of the free, and I
know it. I intend to bear
great fruit."
Oprah Winfrey, 1954 -
American actress and television talk show host

"A closed mind is a dying mind."
Edna Ferber, 1887 - 1968
Playwright and novelist

ROSALYN SUSSMAN YALOW

1921 -

American medical physicist, Rosalyn Sussman Yalow was awarded a share of the 1977 Nobel Prize for Medicine for her development of a procedure called radio-immunoassay (RIA).

While a consultant in nuclear physics for the Bronx Veterans Administration Hospital during the late 1940s, she began investigating various medical applications of radioactive isotopes. By combining techniques from radioisotope tracing and immunology, Yalow developed RIA, which was first applied in studying insulin concentrations in the blood of diabetics, but soon found hundreds of other applications.

In 1976, Rosalyn Sussman Yalow became the first woman to be awarded the Albert Lasker Prize for basic medical research.

"The failure of women to have reached positions of leadership has been due in large part to social and professional discrimination."

"In the past, few women have tried and even fewer have succeeded."

"We still live in a world in which a significant fraction of people, including women, believe that a woman belongs and wants to belong exclusively in the home."

"I'm having trouble managing the mansion. What I need is a wife."
Ella Tambussi Grasso, 1919 - 1989
First woman to become a state governor

"There is a spirit and a need and a man at the beginning of every great human advance. Every one of these must be right for that particular moment of history, or nothing happens."
Coretta Scott King, 1927 -
American lecturer, writer and Civil Rights activist

"Love and respect are the most important aspects of parenting, and of all relationships."
Jodie Foster, 1962 -
American actress

"Don't compromise yourself.
You are all you've got."
Janis Joplin, 1943 - 1970
American singer and songwriter

"It's odd that you can get so
anesthetized by your own pain or
your own problem that you don't
quite fully share the hell of
someone close to you."
Lady Bird Johnson, 1912 -
Former First Lady of the U.S.

"My voice has been raised not only
in song, but to make the big world
outside, through me, understand
something of the spirit of my
beloved country."
Dame Nellie Melba, 1861 - 1931
Australian opera singer

ROSA PARKS
1913 -

Growing up in Montgomery, Ala., Rosa Parks quickly gained firsthand experience with prejudice and inequality. For years she lived with the knowledge that blacks in the South were not entitled to the same rights as those in the North. In 1955, when Rosa Parks refused to give up her seat on a Montgomery bus to a white man, her defiance ignited a bus boycott of 381 days. Rosa Parks' action gave thousands of people the courage to speak out against the injustice toward Southern blacks, furthering the Civil Rights Movement in America.

Rosa Parks continues to influence societal acceptance, co-founding the Rosa and Raymond Parks Institute for Self Development in 1988.

"I'm just an average citizen. Many black people before me were arrested for defying the bus laws. They prepared the way."

"Whatever my individual desires were to be free, I was not alone. There were many others who felt the same way."

"Many whites, even white Southerners, told me that even though it may have seemed like the blacks were being freed, they felt more free and at ease themselves."

"A man's home may seem to be his castle on the outside; inside it is more often his nursery."

Clare Boothe Luce, 1903 - 1987
American diplomat, congresswoman and government official

"Service is what life is all about."

Marion Wright Edelman, 1939 -
American founder and president of the Children's Defense Fund and the first black woman admitted to the Mississippi bar

"Charity separates the rich from the poor; aid raises the needy and sets him on the same level with the rich."

Eva Peron, 1919 - 1952
Argentine politician, government official and lecturer

"I would not be President because I do not aspire to be President but I'm sure that a woman will be President. When? I don't know. It depends. I don't think the woods are full of candidates today."
Ella Tambussi Grasso, 1919 - 1989
First woman to become a state governor

"If I didn't believe the answer could be found, I wouldn't be working on it."
Dr. Florence Sabin, 1871 - 1953
First female professor at a medical school

"Anybody singing the blues is in a deep pit yelling for help."
Mahalia Jackson, 1911 - 1972
American Gospel singer

LOUISA MAY ALCOTT
1832 - 1888

Louisa May Alcott was an American author known for her children's books. She spent most of her life in Boston and Concord, Mass., where she grew up in the company of such literary greats as Ralph Waldo Emerson, Theodore Parker and Henry David Thoreau. Growing up in a Transcendentalist family, Alcott developed a lifelong concern for the welfare of her family. As a young woman, she taught briefly and worked as a domestic to help provide for her parents and three sisters. Eventually, she began to write.

While a nurse during the Civil War, she contracted typhoid from unsanitary hospital conditions and was sent home. She was never completely well again, but the publication of her letters in book form, Hospital Sketches (1863) brought her first taste of fame. Her 1869 book, *Little Women*, was an immediate success. The book described the domestic adventures of a New England family of modest means but optimistic outlook.

"Love is the only thing that we can carry with us when we go, and it makes the end so easy."

"...Love is a great beautifier."

"Far away there in the sunshine are my highest aspirations. I may not reach them, but I can look up and see their beauty, believe in them and try to follow where they lead."

"I postpone death by living, by suffering, by error, by risking, by giving, by loving."
Anais Nin, 1903 - 1985
French/American writer and lecturer

"You take people as far as they will go, not as far as you would like them to go."
Jeannette Rankin, 1880 - 1973
American pacifist, suffragist and congresswoman

"Why not seize the pleasure at once? How often is happiness destroyed by preparation, foolish preparation!"
Jane Austen, 1775 - 1817
English writer

"The one thing that doesn't abide majority rule is a person's conscience."

Harper Lee, 1926 -
American writer and Pulitzer Prize winner

"For loneliness is but cutting adrift from our moorings and floating out to the open sea; an opportunity for finding ourselves, our real selves, what we are about, where we are heading during our little time on this beautiful earth."

Anne Shannon Monroe, 1877 - 1942
American lecturer, novelist and journalist

"The respect that is only bought by gold is not worth much."

Frances E. W. Harper, 1825 - 1911
American lecturer and author

CLARA BARTON
1821 - 1912

Humanitarian and founder of the American Red Cross, Clara Barton was known as "the angel of the battlefield." At the outbreak of the Civil War, she organized an agency to obtain and distribute supplies for the relief of wounded soldiers. In 1865, at the request of President Abraham Lincoln, she set up a bureau of records to aid in the search for missing men. While Barton was in Europe for a rest, she became associated with the International Red Cross, and in 1881 she established the American National Red Cross. The next year, she succeeded in having the U.S. sign the Geneva Agreement on the treatment of sick, wounded and dead in battle and the handling of prisoners of war.

Clara Barton is responsible for the American amendment to the constitution of the Red Cross, which provides for the distribution of relief not only in war but in times of other calamities.

"Everybody's business is nobody's business, and nobody's business is my business."

"It is wise statesmanship which suggests that in time of peace we must prepare for war, and it is no less a wise benevolence that makes preparation in the hour of peace for assuaging the ills that are sure to accompany war."

"Without fanaticism we cannot accomplish anything."
Eva Peron, 1919 - 1952
Argentine politician, government official and lecturer

"The family is the building block for whatever solidarity there is in society."
Jill Ruckelshaus, 1937 -
American government official and lecturer

"Women and elephants never forget."
Dorothy Parker, 1893 - 1967
American writer and poet

"Set the foot down with distrust on the crust of the world—it is thin."
Edna St. Vincent Millay, 1892 - 1950
Poet, playwright and writer

"I don't know anything about luck. I've never banked on it, and I'm afraid of people who do. Luck to me is something else: hard work—and realizing what is opportunity and what isn't."
Lucille Ball, 1911 - 1989
American actress and comedienne

"Art and religion first; then philosophy; lastly science. That is the order of the great subjects of life, their order of importance."
Muriel Spark, 1918 -
Scottish writer and poet

"Beauty is in the eye of the beholder."
Margaret Wolfe Hungerford, 1855 - 1897
Irish writer

SHIRLEY CHISHOLM
1924 -

Shirley Chisholm is the first black woman to have been elected to the U.S. Congress. She served the 12th Congressional District of Brooklyn for seven terms from 1968 until 1982.

In 1972, Chisholm made an unprecedented bid for the Presidential nomination of the Democratic Party, when she received 158 delegate votes. The campaign came one year after she helped co-found the National Women's Political Caucus (NWPC). Designed to mobilize women's political power, the NWPC encourages women to run for political office and endorses those candidates of either sex who support women's rights. She also is the founder and chairwoman of the National Political Congress of Black Women.

In her convictions and courage, Shirley Chisholm lives true to the title of her 1970 autobiography, *Unbought and Unbossed*.

"Tremendous amounts of talent are being lost to our society just because that talent wears a skirt."

"Most Americans have never seen the ignorance, degradation, hunger, sickness and the futility in which many other Americans live... They won't become involved in economic or political change until something brings the seriousness of the situation home to them."

"You don't get to choose how you're going to die, or when. You can only decide how you're going to live. Now!"

Joan Baez, 1941 -
American folksinger and Civil Rights activist

"There is no reason to repeat bad history."

Eleanor Holmes Norton, 1937 -
American lawyer and Civil Rights leader

"It's the friends you can call up at 4 a.m. that matter."

Marlene Dietrich, 1901 - 1992
German actress

"Art is the only way to run away without leaving home."

Twyla Tharp, 1941 -
American choreographer

"When you put your hand to the plow, you can't put it down until you get to the end of the row."
Alice Paul, 1885 - 1977
American author of the Equal Rights Amendment

"As a woman I have no country. As a woman my country is the whole world."
Virginia Woolf, 1882 - 1941
English author

"Love has pride in nothing—but its own humility."
Clare Boothe Luce, 1903 - 1987
American diplomat and congresswoman

"We don't see things as they are, we see them as we are."
Anais Nin, 1903 - 1977
French/American writer and lecturer

EMILY DICKINSON
1830 - 1886

An American poet, Emily Dickinson is recognized as one of the greatest poets of the 19th century. Her verse, along with that of Emerson and Whitman, best defines the distinctive qualities of the American experience.

Emily Dickinson lived intensely, finding in her books, garden and friends the possibilities of rich experience and fulfillment. After her father's death in 1874, she went into the seclusion that led to her being called "the nun of Amherst."

Over a thousand poems were discovered in Emily Dickinson's bureau after her death. In all, she wrote nearly 1,800 poems, several hundred of which are among the finest ever written by any American poet. She gave only 24 of the poems titles, and only seven were published during her lifetime.

"To live is so startling it leaves little time for anything else."

"Success is counted sweetest by those who ne'er succeed."

"Hope is the thing with feathers, that perches in the soul, and sings the tune without the words, and never stops at all."

"If it makes my whole body so cold no fire can warm me, I know it is poetry."

"Thoughts are energy, and you can make your world or break your world by your thinking."
Susan L. Taylor, 1946 -
American journalist

"The freer that women become, the freer will men be. Because when you enslave someone, you are enslaved."
Louise Nevelson, 1900 - 1988
Russian/American sculptor and feminist

"The more I traveled the more I realized that fear makes strangers of people who should be friends."
Shirley MacLaine, 1934 -
American actress and writer

"The human mind can bear plenty of reality, but not too much unintermittent gloom."
Margaret Drabble, 1939 -
English writer

"You can do one of two things; just shut up, which is something I don't find easy, or learn an awful lot very fast, which is what I tried to do."
Jane Fonda, 1937 -
American actress and political activist

"If I'd been a housemaid I'd have been the best in Australia. I couldn't help it. It's got to be perfection for me."
Dame Nellie Melba, 1861 - 1931
Australian opera singer

GLORIA STEINEM
1936 -

Well known as one of the most forceful and articulate campaigners for women's rights, Gloria Steinem assumed the role of a feminist leader in the late 1960s. A journalist, lecturer and television personality, she has used her communication abilities to introduce the general public to issues of the women's liberation movement.

Steinem's most ambitious project involved the 1972 launching of *Ms.*, a nontraditional women's magazine devoted to raising the consciousness of American women. The Toledo, Ohio, native also has been instrumental in founding or directing associations to help end discrimination, such as the National Organization of Women and National Women's Political Caucus.

Through her tireless fundraising, writing and public speaking efforts, Gloria Steinem remains an active political and social critic.

"The new women in politics seem to be saying that we already know how to lose, thank you very much. Now we want to learn how to win."

70

"The first problem for all of us, men and women, is not to learn, but to unlearn."

"Intelligence at the service of poor instinct is really dangerous."

"Sex appeal is 50 percent what you've got, and 50 percent what people think you've got."
Sophia Loren, 1934 -
Italian actress

"I believe in hard work. It keeps the wrinkles out of the mind and the spirit. It helps to keep a woman young."
Helena Rubinstein, 1870 - 1965
American businesswoman and founder of the Helena Rubinstein Foundation

"The world is round and the place which may seem like the end may also be only the beginning."
Ivy Baker Priest, 1905 - 1975
Former U.S. Secretary of the Treasury

"It never occurred to me any more than to a man that I'd stop and turn off my mind because I had children. I think that because I had a strong feeling about what I wanted to do, it enabled me to continue. I never thought of it as unusual."

Sylvia Earle, 1935 -
American marine biologist

"God's gifts put man's best dreams to shame."

Elizabeth Barrett Browning, 1806 - 1861
English poet

"The human heart yearns for the beautiful in all ranks of life."

Harriet Beecher Stowe, 1811 - 1896
American writer and social critic

BABE DIDRIKSON ZAHARIAS
1914 - 1956

American sportswoman Babe Didrikson Zaharias was one of the greatest women athletes, a remarkable performer in basketball, track and field and golf.

In 1930 and 1931, she was a member of the women's All-American basketball team. At the 1932 Olympic Games, she won the gold medals for the 80-meter hurdles and the javelin throw, and was deprived of a third gold medal only because she had used the then unorthodox Western roll in winning the high jump. Zaharias also excelled in baseball, softball, swimming, figure skating, billiards and even football.

She began to golf casually in 1932, but from 1934 on she dedicated herself to the game. Restored to amateur status after several years as a professional, she won the U.S. Women's Amateur tournament in 1946.

Known as much for her skill as her determination, Babe Didrickson Zaharias opened the door to the male-dominated domain of sports.

"All of my life I've always had the urge to do things better than anybody else."

74

"I don't seem able to do my best unless I'm behind or in trouble."

"That little white ball won't move until you hit it, and there's nothing you can do after it has gone."

"Let the world know you as you are, not as you think you should be, because sooner or later, if you are posing, you will forget the pose, and then where are you?"

Fannie Brice, 1891 - 1951
American comedienne and singer

"I like not only to be loved, but to be told that I am loved; the realm of silence is large enough beyond the grave."

George Eliot, 1819 - 1880
English writer

"In passing, also, I would like to say that the first time Adam had a chance, he laid the blame on a woman."

Nancy Astor, 1879 - 1964
British politician

"Character contributes to beauty. It fortifies a woman as her youth fades. A mode of conduct, a standard of courage, discipline, fortitude and integrity can do a great deal to make a woman beautiful."

Jacqueline Bisset, 1946 -
English actress

"In real love you want the other person's good. In romantic love you want the other person."

Margaret Anderson, 1893 - 1973
American writer

"Never go to bed mad. Stay up and fight."

Phyllis Diller, 1917 -
American comedienne

ELIZABETH BLACKWELL
1821 - 1910

In 1849, Elizabeth Blackwell became the first woman in the U.S. to become a physician.

As a young doctor, Blackwell raised funds to open a hospital for needy women and children. During the Civil War, she trained nurses for the Union Army and, in 1868, opened a medical school for women. In 1875, she co-founded a school of medicine for women in England .

Elizabeth Blackwell was a pioneer in the education of women as physicians.

"Medicine is so broad a field, so closely interwoven with general interests, dealing as it does with all ages, sexes and classes, and yet of so personal a character in its individual applications, that it must be regarded as one of those great departments of work in which the cooperation of men and women is needed to fulfill all its requirements."

"It is not easy to be a pioneer—but oh, it is fascinating! I would not trade one moment, even the worst moment, for all the riches in the world."

"For what is done or learned by one class of women becomes, by virtue of their common womanhood, the property of all women."

"I came from a poor and humble background. I did not come from a family of people who had a poverty view of the world. I came from people who viewed the world as attainable."

Faye Wattleton, 1943 -
American nurse and former president of the Planned Parenthood Federation of America

"If you banish fear, nothing terribly bad can happen to you."

Margaret Bourke-White, 1906 - 1971
American photographer

"Faith is the subtle chain which binds us to the infinite."

Elizabeth Oakes Smith, 1806 - 1893
American writer, lecturer and social reformer

"I was always looking outside myself for strength and confidence but it comes from within. It is there all the time."

Anna Freud, 1895 - 1982
Austrian psychotherapist and the daughter of Sigmund Freud

"I say that if each person in this world will simply take a small piece of this huge thing, this tablecloth, bedspread, whatever, and work on it regardless of the color of the yarn, we will have harmony on this planet."

Cicely Tyson, 1933 -
American actress

PEARL S. BUCK
1892 - 1973

An author noted for her novels of life in China, Pearl S. Buck was the recipient of the Nobel Prize for Literature in 1938. She spent her youth in China, where her parents were Presbyterian missionaries.

Buck received her early education in Shanghai and returned to teach at a Chinese university after graduating from a Virginia women's college in 1914. Her articles and stories about Chinese life first appeared in U.S. magazines in 1923, but it was not until 1931 that she reached a wide audience with *The Good Earth*.

After World War II, to aid illegitimate children of U.S. servicemen in Asian countries, she instituted the Pearl S. Buck Foundation. To this organization she donated more than $7 million of her personal earnings.

"Every great mistake has a halfway moment, a split second when it can be recalled and perhaps remedied."

"One faces the future with one's past."

"Hunger makes a thief of any man."

"When hope is taken away from the people, moral degeneration follows swiftly after."

"You must learn to be still in the midst of activity, and to be vibrantly alive in repose."
Indira Gandhi, 1917 - 1984
Prime Minister of India

"In my younger days, when I was pained by the half-educated, loose and inaccurate ways women had, I used to say, 'How much women need exact science.' But since I have known some workers in science, I have now said, 'How much science needs women.'"
Maria Mitchell, 1818 - 1889
First woman astronomer in the U.S. and the first woman member of the American Academy of Arts and Sciences Hall of Fame

"The environment that people live in is the environment that they learn to live in, respond to and perpetuate. If the environment is good, so be it. But if it is poor, so is the quality of life within it."

Ellen Swallow Richards, 1842 - 1911
American chemist and ecologist

"Measure not the work until the day's out and the labor done."

Elizabeth Barret Browning, 1806 - 1861
English poet

"The only reason I would take up jogging is so that I could hear heavy breathing again."

Erma Bombeck, 1927 - 1996
American humorist and writer

WILMA RUDOLPH
1940 - 1994

One of 22 children, Wilma Rudolph grew up in Tennessee. Stricken with polio at an early age, Wilma believed she would one day walk again without braces because of her mother's inspiration.

At the age of nine, the braces were removed and Rudolph spent all of her free time running and at play. In the years that followed, she was extremely active in basketball and track. Her years of dedication were rewarded in 1960 at the Olympic Games in Rome. She was the first woman to win three gold medals in track and field. Today, Wilma Rudolph passes on her skill and determination as the Track Director and Special Consultant on Minority Affairs at DePauw University in Greencastle, Ind.

"My mother was the one who made me work, made me believe that one day it would be possible for me to walk without braces."

"Sometimes it takes years to really grasp what has happened to your life."

86

"I've been asked to run as a pro, but my interests now are my family...and the kids I'm working with. Now I'm trying to develop other champions."

"My life has been a tapestry of rich and royal hue, an everlasting vision of the everchanging view."
Carole King, 1941 -
American singer and songwriter

"Independence I have long considered the grand blessing of life, the basis of every virtue."
Mary Wollstonecraft, 1759 - 1797
American feminist

"Everybody wants to do something to help, but nobody wants to be first."
Pearl Bailey, 1918 - 1990
American singer

"Boredom helps one to make decisions."
Colette, 1873 - 1954
French writer

"I do not believe in sex distinction in literature, law, politics or trade—or that modesty and virtue are more becoming to women than men."

Belva Lockwood, 1830-1917
First woman to practice law before the Supreme Court

"I think that education is power. I think that being able to communicate with people is power. One of my main goals on the planet is to encourage people to empower themselves."

Oprah Winfrey, 1954 -
American actress and television talk show host

"We're all in this alone."

Lily Tomlin, 1936 -
American comedienne and actress

KATHARINE HEPBURN
1909 -

Katharine Hepburn, as a young woman, became an instant success on the American stage and in motion pictures. From the start, she was a spirited performer with a touch of Yankee eccentricity. Unafraid of challenges, Hepburn has commonly taken courageous political stands and accepted roles that test her acting ability. She introduced into film a strength of character previously considered undesirable in Hollywood leading ladies.

A role model for women throughout the world, she is noted for her brisk New England accent, unique style and rare beauty. Winner of four Academy Awards, Katharine Hepburn is a witty, independent woman who remains one of the most beloved actresses in America.

"I can remember walking as a child. It was not customary to say you were fatigued. It was customary to complete the goal of the expedition."

"Plain women know more about men than beautiful ones do."

"To keep your character intact you cannot stoop to filthy acts. It makes it easier to stoop the next time."

"Without discipline, there's no life at all."

"Never turn down a job because you think it's too small, you don't know where it can lead."

Julia Morgan, 1872 - 1957
American architect

"For women there are, undoubtedly, great difficulties in the path, but so much the more to overcome. First, no woman should say, 'I am but a woman!' But a woman? What more can you ask to be?"

Maria Mitchell, 1818 - 1889
First woman astronomer in the U.S. and the first woman member of the American Academy of Arts and Sciences Hall of Fame

"Reality is something you rise above."

Liza Minnelli, 1946 -
American actress and singer

"Some people are moulded by their admirations, others by their hostilities."
Elizabeth Bowen, 1899 - 1973
Anglo/Irish author

"Parents, however old they and we may grow to be, serve among other things to shield us from a sense of our doom. As long as they are around, we can avoid the fact of our mortality; we can still be innocent children."
Jane Howard, 1935 -
American writer

"For fast-acting relief try slowing down."
Lily Tomlin, 1936 -
American comedienne and actress

MARGARET CHASE SMITH
1897 - 1995

Maine native Margaret Chase Smith began her political career in 1930, when at the age of 33 she became a member of the Republican State Committee.

In 1940, Smith was elected to the 77th Congress. The independent-thinking Congresswoman from Maine served eight years in the House of Representatives until she was elected to the U.S. Senate in 1948.

Margaret Chase Smith's honest, straightforward way gained her widespread popularity across the country and serious consideration to be America's first female vice presidential candidate.

"The key to security is public information. Before you can become a statesman you first have to get elected, and to get elected you have to be a politician pledging support for what the voters want."

"I believe that in our constant search for security we can never gain any peace of mind until we secure our own soul."

"The critical responsibility for the generation you're in is to help provide the shoulders, the direction and the support for those generations who come behind."

Gloria Dean Randle Scott, 1938 -
President of Bennett College, North Carolina

"It's so clear that you have to cherish everyone. I think that's what I get from these older black women, that every soul is to be cherished, that every flower is to bloom."

Alice Walker, 1944 -
Novelist and winner of the Pulitzer Prize for Fiction

"The first rule in opera is the first rule in life; see to everything yourself."
Dame Nellie Melba, 1861 - 1931
Australian opera singer

"This became a credo of mine: Attempt the impossible in order to improve your work."
Bette Davis, 1908 - 1991
American actress

"If you want a place in the sun, you've got to put up with a few blisters."
Abigail Van Buren, 1918 -
American newspaper columnist and lecturer

WILMA PEARL MANKILLER
1945 -

Wilma Pearl Mankiller spent her early years on a Cherokee farm in Oklahoma, where she first became concerned with the mistreatment of the Cherokee Nation.

An activist for Indian rights, Mankiller believed that the Cherokees themselves knew how best to resolve their own problems. She worked with the Indian people to improve living conditions and create opportunity.

Mankiller became the first woman deputy chief and, in 1985, the Principal Chief of the Cherokee Nation. Today she governs some 120,000 people of the second largest Indian nation in the U.S.

Promoting education, jobs and farming, Chief Wilma Mankiller's determined way is restoring Cherokee communities.

"I've run into more discrimination as a woman than as an Indian."

She likened her job to "running a small country, a medium corporation, and being a social worker."

"A lot of young girls have looked to their career paths and have said they'd like to be chief. There's been a change in the limits people see."

"If our American way of life fails the child, it fails us all."

Pearl S. Buck, 1892 - 1973
American author and recipient of the Nobel Prize for Literature in 1938

"I am for lifting everyone off the social bottom. In fact, I am for doing away with the social bottom altogether."

Clare Boothe Luce, 1903 - 1987
American diplomat and congresswoman

"To me success means effectiveness in the world, that I am able to carry my ideas and values into the world—that I am able to change it in positive ways."

Maxine Hong Kingston, 1940 -
Writer and professor

"If you really want to reach for the brass ring, just remember that there are sacrifices that go along."
Cathleen Black, 1944
American businesswoman, president of Hearst Magazine:

"Mistakes are a fact of life. It is the response to error that counts."
Nikki Giovanni, 1943 -
American poet

"I tell myself that God gave my children many gifts—spirit, beauty, intelligence, the capacity to make friends and to inspire respect. There was only one gift he held back—length of life."
Rose Kennedy, 1890 - 1995
Mother of President John F. Kennedy

MARGARET MITCHELL
1900 - 1949

American author Margaret Mitchell was raised in Georgia. As the daughter of the president of the Atlanta Historical Society, she developed an intense interest in local history.

From this background, Mitchell started to write a novel of the Civil War and Reconstruction from a Southern point of view, transforming the stories she remembered from her childhood. After 10 years and over 1,000 pages, *Gone With the Wind* was published in 1935. The novel won the Pulitzer Prize and the National Book Award. *Gone With the Wind* set a record in publishing history, selling 50,000 copies in one day. It has been translated into 30 languages.

Margaret Mitchell will be remembered for the book behind one of the most popular films ever made.

"Life's under no obligation to give us what we expect. We take what we get and are thankful it's no worse than it is."

"What most people don't seem to realize is that there is just as much money to be made out of the wreckage of civilization as from the upbuilding of one."

"Death and taxes and childbirth: There's never any convenient time for any of them!"

"The oppressed never free themselves—they do not have the necessary strengths."
Clare Boothe Luce, 1903 - 1987
American diplomat and congresswoman

"Anger repressed can poison a relationship as surely as the cruelest words."
Joyce Brothers, 1925 -
American psychologist and writer

"It's the good girls who keep the diaries; the bad girls never have the time."
Tallulah Bankhead, 1903 - 1968
American actress

"A woman today has to do more than her male counterpart. Come in knowing that you're going to have to give 200 percent effort to get 100 percent credit. And most of the time you will get 100 percent credit."

Sherian Grace Codoria, 1940 -
Brigadier General, highest-ranking black woman in the U.S. Armed Forces and one of only four female army generals

"Whoever said, 'It's not whether you win or lose that counts,' probably lost."

Martina Navratilova, 1956 -
Professional tennis player

FLORENCE NIGHTINGALE
1820 - 1910

An English nurse, Florence Nightingale was the founder of trained nursing for women. While in charge of nursing at a Turkish military hospital during the Crimean War (1854 - 1856), she coped with overcrowding, poor sanitation and a shortage of basic medical supplies. As Nightingale made her nightly hospital rounds she gave comfort and advice, establishing the image of "The Lady with the Lamp" among the wounded.

Regarded as an expert on public hospitals, she was dedicated to improving the health and living conditions of the British soldier. In 1860, she founded the Nightingale School for Nurses, the first such school of its kind and the world.

Florence Nightingale has been immortalized as the epitome of tender care.

"I can stand out the war with any man."

"I stand at the altar of the murdered men, and while I live, I fight their cause."

"I never lose an opportunity of urging a practical beginning, however small, for it is wonderful how often the mustard seed germinates and roots itself."

"The more the wonders of the world become inaccessible, the more intensely do its curiosities affect us."
Colette, 1873 - 1954
French writer

"Honor wears different coats to different eyes."
Barbara Tuchman, 1912 - 1989
American historian and Pulitzer Prize winner

"Like the resource it seeks to protect, wildlife conservation must be dynamic, changing as conditions change, seeking always to become more effective."
Rachel Carson, 1907 - 1964
American marine biologist and environmentalist

"We were united by common bond of interest. We spoke each other's language—and that was the language of pioneer women of the air." [Discussing her relationship with Amelia Earhart.]

Ruth Rowland Nichols, 1901 - 1961
American aviator and first woman to pilot a passenger airplane

"If we get a government that reflects more of what this country is really about, we can turn the century—and the economy— around."

Bella Abzug, 1920 -
American congresswoman and lawyer

CLARA McBRIDE HALE
1905 - 1992

A devoted and loving mother, Clara McBride Hale raised her own children along with more than 30 other youngsters. Her unconditional love for children led this remarkable woman to open Hale House in Harlem, N. Y., during the early 1970s.

Hale House was a desperately needed center for infants born to drug-addicted mothers. In the midst of poverty, this program provided nurturing, love and medical attention to those helpless babies of families who also received care and rehabilitation. The legacy of this extraordinary woman lives on in the current administrator of the Hale House, Dr. Lorraine Hale, Clara McBride Hale's daughter.

In 1985, "Mother" Clara McBride Hale was named an "American hero" by President Ronald Reagan.

"Until I die, I'm going to keep doing. My people need me. They need somebody that's not taking from them and is giving them something."

"I'm not an American hero. I'm a person who loves children."

"Being black does not stop you. You can sit out in the world and say, 'Well, white people kept me back, and I can't do this.' Not so. You can have anything you want if you make up your mind and you want it."

"My address is like my shoes. It travels with me. I abide where there is a fight against wrong."
Mother Jones, 1830 - 1930
Irish/American labor organizer and humanitarian

"Always the edge of the sea remains an elusive and indefinable boundary. The shore has a dual nature, changing with the swing of the tides, belonging now to the land, now to the sea."
Rachel Carson, 1907 - 1964
American marine biologist and environmentalist

"You have put me in here [jail] a cub, but I will come out roaring like a lion."
Carry Nation, 1846 - 1911
American prohibitionist

"Labour: to feel with one's whole self the existence of the world. Love: to feel with one's whole self the existence of another being." [Commenting on physical love and labour.]
Simone Weil, 1910 - 1943
French theologian, philosopher, journalist and scholar

"Parents have become so convinced that educators know what is best for children that they forget that they themselves are really experts."
Marion Wright Edelman, 1939 -
Founder of the Children's Defense Fund, Civil Rights activist and the first black woman admitted to the bar in Mississippi

ELIZABETH CADY STANTON

1815 - 1902

Raised in New York, Elizabeth Cady Stanton learned at a young age about discrimination against women. She studied law with her father, Judge Daniel Cady, but was refused admission to the bar because of her sex. Angered by discrimination and legal restrictions against women, Stanton became involved in antislavery and temperance movements. In 1848, she was an organizer of the Seneca Falls Convention, where she was the first to call for a woman's right to vote. In 1851, Stanton convinced Susan B. Anthony to join the women's rights movement. Together, these two women worked for female suffrage and expanded rights.

As president of the National Woman Suffrage Association, Elizabeth Cady Stanton helped lay the foundation and developed ideas that would become the platforms of the women's rights movement.

"Reformers who are always compromising, have not yet grasped the idea that truth is the only safe ground to stand upon."

"To throw obstacles in the way of a complete education is like putting out the eyes."

"Nothing strengthens the judgment and quickens the conscience like individual responsibility."

"I deplore any action which denies artistic talent an opportunity to express itself because of prejudice against race origin."
Bess Truman, 1885 - 1982
Former First Lady of the U.S.

"I don't mind if my life goes in the service of the nation. If I die, every drop of my blood will invigorate the nation."
Indira Gandhi, 1917 - 1984
Prime Minister of India

"I felt a comedy ego beginning to grow, which gave me the courage to begin tentatively looking into myself for material."
Joan Rivers, 1933 -
American comedienne and television talk show host

"The legacy I want to leave is a child-care system that says that no kid is going to be left alone or left unsafe."

Marion Wright Edelman, 1939 -
Founder of the Children's Defense Fund, Civil Rights activist and the first black woman admitted to the bar in Mississippi

"We are stardust, we are golden, and we've got to get ourselves back to the garden."

Joni Mitchell, 1943 -
American singer and songwriter

"There is only one real sin and that is to persuade oneself that the second-best is anything but second best."

Doris Lessing, 1919 -
English author

AMELIA EARHART
1898 - 1937?

An American aviator, Amelia Earhart was the first woman to fly solo across the Atlantic Ocean.

After a Kansas upbringing and education, she learned to fly in California, taking up aviation as a hobby. Following a series of record flights, she made a solo transatlantic flight from Harbour Grace, Newfoundland, to Ireland and later flew the first solo from Hawaii to the American mainland.

In June 1937, Earhart attempted the first round-the-world flight near the equator. After taking off on July 1 from New Guinea for Howland Island in the Pacific, her plane vanished. A great naval search failed to locate her and it was assumed that she had been lost at sea.

The mystery and fascination surrounding Amelia Earhart's life and death continue to the current day.

"Courage is the price that life exacts for granting peace. The soul that knows it not, knows no release from little things."

"Adventure is worthwhile in itself."

"In soloing—as in other activities—it is far easier to start something than to finish it."

"There are two kinds of stones, as everyone knows, one of which rolls."

"The only causes of regret are laziness, outbursts of temper, hurting others, prejudice, jealousy and envy."

Germaine Greer, 1939 -
Australian author and educator

"If we could sell our experiences for what they cost us, we'd all be millionaires."

Abigail Van Buren, 1918 -
American newspaper columnist and lecturer

"Expect trouble as an inevitable part of life and repeat to yourself the most comforting words of all: This, too, shall pass."

Ann Landers, 1918 -
American newspaper columnist

"The one thing that doesn't abide by majority rule is a person's conscience."

Harper Lee, 1926 -
American writer and Pulitzer Prize winner

"I have great belief in the fact that whenever there is chaos, it creates wonderful thinking. I consider chaos a gift."

Septima Poinsette Clark, 1898 - 1987
American Civil Rights activist

"Something which we think is impossible now is not impossible in another decade."

Constance Baker Motley, 1921 -
First black woman to become a federal judge in the U.S.

GOLDA MEIR
1898 - 1978

Golda Meir was a founder of the State of Israel, and served as its fourth prime minister. Born in Kiev, Ukraine, she emigrated to Wisconsin in 1906. Her political activity began as a leader in the Milwaukee Labor Zionist Party.

After emigrating to Palestine in 1921, she held key posts in the Jewish Agency and in the World Zionist Organization. After Israel proclaimed its independence in 1948, she served as minister of labor, and then foreign minister. Meir was appointed prime minister in 1969.

During her administration, she worked for a peace settlement in the Middle East using diplomatic means. She resigned her post in 1974, but remained an important political figure throughout her retirement.

Golda Meir's true strength and spirit were emphasized when, after her death in 1978, it was revealed that she had suffered from leukemia for 12 years.

"A leader who doesn't hesitate before he sends his nation into battle is not fit to be a leader."

"You cannot shake hands with a clenched fist."

"I can honestly say that I was never affected by the question of the success of an undertaking. If I felt it was the right thing to do, I was for it regardless of the possible outcome."

"The will to be totally rational is the will to be made out of glass and steel—and to use others as if they were glass and steel."

Marge Piercy, 1936 -
Founder of the Movement for a Democratic Society

"People change and forget to tell each other."

Lillian Hellman, 1907 - 1984
American playwright and writer

"To be somebody, a woman does not have to be more like a man, but has to be more of a woman."

Sally E. Shaywitz, 1942 -
American pediatrician and writer

"Spirit is the real and eternal; matter is the unreal and temporal."

Mary Baker Eddy, 1821 - 1910
Founder of the Christian Science religion

"Our school education ignores, in a thousand ways, the rules of healthy development."

Elizabeth Blackwell, 1820 - 1910
First American woman physician

"You should always know when you're shifting gears in life. You should leave your era; it should never leave you."

Leontyne Price, 1927 -
American opera singer and recipient of 18 Grammy Awards

"You can't invent events. They just happen. But you have to be prepared to deal with them when they happen."

Constance Baker Motley, 1921 -
First black woman to become a federal judge in the U.S.

Index

POWERFUL INSIGHTS TO IMPROVE
YOUR CAREER, YOUR BUSINESS, YOUR LIFE.

Successories, Inc. 1-800-535-2773